carrying place

carrying place

poems

esta spalding

Anansi

Copyright © 1995 by Esta Spalding

All rights reserved. No part of this publication may be reproduced or transmitted in any form or by any means, electronic or mechanical, including photocopying, recording, or any information storage and retrieval system, without permission in writing from the publisher.

Published in 1995 by
House of Anansi Press Limited
1800 Steeles Avenue West
Concord, Ontario
L4K 2P3
Tel.(416)445-3333
Fax (416)445-5967

Canadian Cataloguing in Publication Data
Spalding, Esta
Carrying place
Poems.
ISBN 0-88784-568-1
I. Title
PS8587.P35C37 1995   C811'.54   C95-930324-3
PR9199.3.S73C37 1995

Cover design: the boy 100 and Tannice Goddard
Author photograph: Michael Ondaatje
Editing: Anne Szumigalski

Printed and bound in Canada

House of Anansi Press gratefully acknowledges the support of the Canada Council, the Ontario Ministry of Culture, Tourism, and Recreation, Ontario Arts Council, and Ontario Publishing Centre in the development of writing and publishing in Canada.

for my mother

Contents

First Place

Border *3*
Belonging to You *4*
Eggs *5*
The Cow *7*
Return *9*
Salt *11*
The Castle *12*
The Application *13*
Under the Blankets *14*
Afterwards *15*
Pigeons *17*
Backyard Growing Up *19*
Orgasm, Age 12 *21*
Ladies of the Dam *22*
Bread *23*

Touched

Alexander Supertramp *27*
Leaving the Fundamental
 Assumptions Unexpressed *30*
Torn *31*
Touched *33*
Pinned *35*
Welfare Blues *37*
Twin *38*
Long Distance *40*
Carrying Place *41*
Fall *42*
Dog Notes *44*
Unravelling *45*

Then 46
The Cell 47
The Split 49
Snapshot 51
Epaulettes 52
Loosestrife 53

Love's Back

After the Drought 57
Your Touch 58
Early Morning 59
But Only the Captains of This Earth 60
Broad Reach 61
Love's Back 62
Storm Room 63
Detail from Storm Room 64
Detail from Detail from Storm Room 65
Mercury, a Quick Note to You 66
Scales 68
What the Cookbook Doesn't Say 70
Moving In 71
How I Came to Know the Woman in Him 72
Fractal Lover 74
Daughter Imagined 75
Le Rêve 76
Shipbuilding 77
My Epileptic 78
Airborne 79
North 80

Notes 83
Acknowledgements 85

deep
in the green sea
I saw two sides of the water
and swam between them

— *W. S. Merwin*

FIRST PLACE

Border

My parents observe the helmeted man
pulled from the car, his leather
skin smoking, his body a fuse.
My mother was married on Memorial Day
during the Indy 500,
and her memories of my father are clouded
by an image of salvage:
                        a man pulled from a wreck.

He came to her in college through the cracked-open
window of her dorm. When she found him later
he was drunk on the mariachis and salt of Mexico
on the other side of a border
he had named. He fell
into her arms and slept, waking to sing
the song of liberation that told her name,
Cielito Lindo.

She rescued him again
from the Vietnam collision,
giving him the child I became
effecting the pull from her own body.

Ask me about gametes, the cells,
half-empty,
half-full of chromosomes,
I will speak with the completeness
of one salvaged
from parts on migration. I speak
from fetal country.
Each gamete a window open to a stranger.

Belonging to You
for Philip Spalding

Entering the sea that spoke your name,
I don't have much to recommend me:
your dental work,
a knowledge of geology,
and an urge to wet my feet in your body.

But I am startled by the stones.
I didn't think it would be so hard
to be your daughter, or so hard
to share your name. Your Celtic
name that means *breaking rocks*.

Your friend's son had a stone caught
in his throat.
You knew the nerves and pushed
on the child's foot; the rock became
his first metamorphic sound.

These rocks are the tide's refusal
spit on to sand, like the teeth, beer,
and blood knocked down
your throat in the broken
dialect of a fight with a man
who cursed your name.

What sentence will I find here
in the bitching sea whose rocks
wreck my interpretations?
With my ankles in the water, I leave
my luck in the press
of your palms,
spalding your name on my tongue.

Eggs

My mother cracks eggs
into the cast iron skillet.
Taps them on the edge
then thrusting thumb into crack
pulls out their jelly insides.
How do you want them?
We are on stools, toes pointed
at the cracks between linoleum slabs.
We won't step on those.
Scrambled, poached?
Kristin spins through air
like a whisk in milk
        outside the low belch of septic tank
she says, *I'll never brush my hair again.*
It hangs a pale web around her neck.
Where do eggs come from?

When she was born
I painted my body black,
waited on the steps for the car to come home,
when she emerged pink and glazed
I clutched her to blackness,
anointed, immaculate.
Marks on my body where hers had been.

From birds, my mother says.
I wait, like I waited for the pork chop
to cook in my Betty Crocker oven,
came back days later to find a plate
of maggots I had made from meat.
Their bodies, tiny fingers

the colour of cream. I grew
them in my oven: a whole
box of maggots
that ate until they grew wings.

We are in the kitchen spinning,
legs wide open.

I can raise the dead.

The Cow

What was the cow we found
dead beside the split-wood fence?
What door was this slab of hide?
When we lifted the skin lid
the body crawled with organs.
Sark took a stick to move the insides
and we studied the roaming entrails —
my arm propping open the skin,
the raw backs of our necks brushing its underside,
and the maggots whose suck was
the music of cow decay, the decomposing.

We crawled into that body, Sark and I,
our own small animal selves
entered the cow's belly, her blue skull,
and the empty eyes,
those channels of power
that had propelled her
towards the rich world of grass.

That summer, when Sark slid from the hood of our jeep
onto the dirt and the stone,
under the slice of my father's tire,
I held him in my arms
for the sixteen miles, the eight locked gates
that separated us from a telephone.
His eyes peeled back from his skull,
the lashes fluttering against his lip,
I cradled the body-sack of my brother
wanting to hold the pain for him, to taste the lashes
that brushed the lip, eyeball

that could only see the inside things,
and me in a bikini with this bleeding firstborn in my arms.
I blame the cow
who lied to us about death's pleasure,
who fooled our maggot hearts.

Return

The island's angles and elbows
as familiar to me as the brown bodies
of my brothers and sister
squeezed together and pressed
against the windows of my father's car
as it coasted down the highway
in neutral (to save gas) and we
slid over the plastic seats
like an eight-armed creature found waiting
in tide pools
for the break that would carry it
beyond bounds.

Driving again the old road around the island,
I trace the limits,
stalking its circumference: the Pali Road
was dry on the windward side, but sweeping
through the tunnel into Honolulu
we would enter a new, wet
world; on the Swamp Road, a mermaid mannequin
hung from the trees like a siren
between the abandoned bodies
of the cars where men and wild dogs lived.

Again at the light on Oneawa Street,
at the intersection with jabbering birds,
a huge banyan tree,
where we waited every morning for the bus
holding our books, cellos, and surfboards.
We knew the distance between bus stops
by the rhythm of tires on slick roads.

For this moment, like a strange dream whose language
makes sense only within itself, whose edges

dim with consciousness — for this moment only,
all four bodies start,
stop, stretch,
and return.

Salt
for Sark

thrown past the dash
board   in neutral   no gas
six-pack between your legs
we bumped   dropped
free fall
down Wilhelmina Rise
in a four-wheel-drive
ford   the Pacific below

do you still drive like you surf
an artist of thrill and slice
suturing skin of tube, asphalt gut?

after all these years, it's your heart
that pulls me over the hills

if i could dry you
like sea on rocks,
i'd carry you with me: a salt rodeo,
bucking horses   trucks
striking road and rise

The Castle

The day my father dug a home for us
in the sand, a house two feet deep
with a shifting foundation.
The day he picked me up
from the other home, green like a lingering bruise,
with concrete floors my mother poured,
that day my father suffered for me,
spent all afternoon in the sun,
dug with aching arms, through crab bite
and coral cut, the sweat breaking
on his forehead, surf in a storm.
At twilight he led me through:
Here is your kitchen with shelves for storing food.
Here is your living room.
He had carved a television set in the side of a cliff,
bright shells for knobs and dials.
A table, an oven, a bed.
Don't wipe your feet when you come in.
The sun was falling on the horizon
bright with red streaks. *Where will you sleep?* I asked.
Because I loved him
who had spent the day with his back to me
and I loved the house he had built,
and in the last blank burning rays of sun
I turned greedy to him
and begged, *keep me.*

The Application

The application my mother wrote
to The School of Social Work,
the creased, brown wrinkles
I've discovered left in an old book.
I know we replicate cells, exchanging
an old body for a new one every seven years,
how do we hold ourselves together?
> *My husband and I have just been through*
> *marriage counselling — I want to help*
> *other families like ours.*

She has already shed the skin of these words.
What fell from her when she was my age, twenty-four,
cautious, untouched?
> *We have two children,*
> *one four, the other two.*
> *My husband works nights*
> *feeding pigeons. It's hard for him,*
> *he has to sleep with the first*
> *light . . .*

In six months her father would die,
her husband would leave her for a pregnant girl.
She sits in the afternoon light,
alone at a table, bare
except for the typewriter she has borrowed
to type this application.
She hasn't heard me —
bent, silent
touching her paper skin.

Under the Blankets

Her body is a moon, a sickle,
is to be picked up and swung,
to be rung — the pealing,
the tongues of the resurrection
licking the side of my sister's body
awake in bed next to mine,
we always sleep together
and I am twelve years old and she is nine,
and where is hers and whose is hers
or which is mine.
I can't find the seam between us.

We are in the womb, under blankets,
hiding from chilly rooms
where we will separate.

Afterwards

While I went to school in a bright classroom,
she was shut in the attic
across the street.
We learned about it afterwards
and could never look
at painted glass the same way.

We made my mother tell it
over and over — how the grandmother
rescued her out of a window
in the house where the mother and father
had given themselves to a man
who said the girl needed to be sealed.

The parents were free
to work and eat, to give
their earnings to the man
and take food from his table.
The girl had too much power.

Alone in the room for a year and a half —
alone in the room counting, naming sounds that passed.

My mother told me she could hear
our voices in the classroom across the street.
She knew our names.
She trained herself to listen.
When we spoke of Africa, Greece,
when we read about the Czar's daughter
in history books,
she was painted into her room.

And afterwards, my sister and I would fall asleep
imagining we might have rescued her
with nail files and string.

We stared at windows.

Pigeons

In the beginning she trusted him,
he, her.
The pale
slant of light
on the floor soaked
the wood grains till they glowed.
The light fell through
the blinds in slivers and pieces
like needles or feathers.
I want to go back to the room
where he told her
he would sell his blood
for the babies breathing
in the crib. He would let
his blood.
He, who had made them from himself
in the first place,
he, who would one day leave them,
he was saying that he would open his veins
to nurse.

The light on the floor breaks
into pieces, feathered light
piercing the babies
asleep in the crib. He took a job
feeding pigeons in a laboratory
to keep the babies full, to pay
for the room where light
scattered like wings in an aviary.

Opening my notebook here
where sunlight is cheap,
this room with space and time
to breathe, a room

without fear,
I want to go back
because he opened himself,
his blood bought this.

Bend back the spine
of the book. Release
wings beating.

Backyard Growing Up

She planted the *be still tree*
over the septic tank. It grew red,
vibrant with waste's luxury. Every Saturday
it was trimmed, the whole lawn raked,
in a ceremony of what's commonplace.

Twice a week we ate fast-food specials: hotdogs,
fries, root beer, one dollar. We spun
in the plastic chairs, our tanned colt's legs
hanging over the edge, our arms thrust out
like blades, we sang: *I walked one morning
by the sea and all the waves reached out to me.*
My mother made us share our fries.

Sometimes we only bought seventy-two cents
worth of gas. Sometimes we had bad dreams.

We sang loud and wanted nothing.
When I was twelve she bought me a rose bush.
Every week a new bud appeared, a jewel
made from dirt.

Was I the weeds we learned to name
in school: *welfare rose, showy tick,
bastard poppy, loosestrife?*

My mother combing my hair
as I ran for the bus to school
or making leis on May Day
with blossoms from the backyard.

At night, my sister and I prayed
to the Cricketman

asking for the chance to sing,
for louder voices,
the *be still tree* below our window.

Orgasm, Age 12

In the dream, my brother and I fall
into the V of a valley
with too much rain.
We are alone and though I know
I am responsible
for the care of his body,
though I must respond to the fall,
I can't remember what the answer is.
We are plummeting
wrapped in mist,
the two of us, brother
and sister, in a world of edges,
like the cartoon coyote,
we are surprised by mid-air.

In the breaking of the dream
I realize my stiff back
and my angry neck
are the strain of wings
if I can use them.

I arch till
my backbones are taut
to the wind,
each feather stiff
clutching space. I pull
my brother into the cradle
of my arms,
into sleep.
No more valleys
of too much rain,
no more cries for foothold.

Ladies of the Dam
for Raymond Souster

It was the year psychics said
Janis Joplin would be First Lady.
We were standing on the *crazy-high*
railroad bridge, trying to touch
the edge of water that pushed itself over
the barrier of the dam. Kristin was
on the tips of her toes tilting,
testing, wishing she hadn't bitten her fingernails,
the water breathed so close. If only we could reach
beyond the rail into what was hidden
behind the quick sheets of water.

We wanted to be older, taller,
but weren't ready to straighten
our parts, or to be ladies.

Will they believe us if we reach it?

Kristin lifted her calloused feet
into my palms, body loaded
like a gun. I staggered forward
till her knees kissed the metal
and she leaned over the rail,
her tense form its own cascade.
Slowly she reached out, searching,
thirsty, pressing her palms through water,
put on silver gloves.

Bread

Who says the body's only 2/3 water?
What myth was told to us?
In the swimming pool with all of you
there was no separation of solid and liquid.
We sublimated, moving between
your skin and mine, your mucus and mine.
Our heavier parts shed themselves,
a chemical reaction, temperature rising.
On the horizontal together.
Where else do bodies meet on this plane?

My shoulders ached at the end of a day: the ball
and socket having ground, oh, the flour
we milled, the butter churned,
a whole city lit by the motion of arching arms,
by the snap of tendons, and the beating
of all those hearts, a factory of hearts!

The swimmer is pure and Godly number,
the mathematics of pull and torque,
pace, angle, breath, lap, turns,
the time between intervals and sets.
(The bubbles that shouldn't have been on my fingertips,
I carried too much air in my hands!) And the meter:
there was the record I broke in the quad cities
swimming my 500 in 3/4 time
to the rhythms of Muddy Waters,
angry and blue, and me a Chicago Girl —
what music was in this labour!

I toast you
Kris Novak who dove into Wenniger's puke,
finishing the race anyway,

and Tord Alshabkhoun who said
Rotate your torso. Read the backstroke flag.
Coach Fober, for throwing kickboards
when I thought my legs were through,
and for the eternal fishtail
in a crummy van
on slick Midwestern roads.
You drove us from one corn town to the next.

Thanks, because my body
isn't a border, and water isn't the baptism,
that was a myth too; it's the holy meal,
bread of a thousand.

TOUCHED

Alexander Supertramp

for Christopher McCandless
who called himself Alexander Supertramp

I
The bus is a cold body when I first arrive.
Ten days of hitchhiking to the Great White North, here's
freedom. I will be immaculate, unknowable.
I will shed all twenty-four years
as I have shed my family, their money.
I will be a pure thing: backpack,
Remington Nylon 66 semiautomatic,
ten-pound bag of rice.

What kind of small game can I kill?
What kind of berries, eat?

The Fairbanks Transit bus is
freedom of silence, freedom of self.
I forage from here, moving
outside the shelter of this mother wreck.

II
At night I watch the moon cut the hard edge of things,
I mark my nights in a book — it is
the nights that purify, the nights
that take my weight off, scouring me,
winnowing out the heavy parts. I have no weight
here in the 49th state, I have been sifted.

Arriving here, I crossed the frozen Teklanika River,
solid, it held its pieces together.
But the moon will loosen this river too.
I am here a month
when the river begins to thaw.
I have no map.

III
In May, I find little to hunt: some squirrels,
some ducks and grouse, but I am more and more
hungry, and the days which are for filling what the nights
    will take
give little. I see a grizzly, but I cannot shoot,
I will not shoot the bear.
I am reading what I would consume: Tolstoy,
Thoreau, *The Terminal Man*, a book on plants.

Later, when I am starving, I kill a moose.
This is an act the night cannot forgive.
The mountains I climb in apology. I work six days
to preserve the meat,
but there are mosquitoes now, and flies.
I carve holes in the dirt
to smoke the carcass, boil the entrails in a stew,
but maggots grow; the flies have spread themselves
into the future — this is my tragedy, this is my crime —
the moon drags over me in inquisition.

Henceforth will learn to accept my errors, however great they be —
In the death of the moose, I have pared down,
I am thing now, sickle of thin moon
that maggots eat,
and I can say pure words: bus, river, pitcher, pack.
I can live pure words: gun, root.

Though I am starving, I will not burn the forest.

IV
family happiness
I am ready to leave the inside of the bus, to expurgate,
patch jeans, shave!, organize pack
I am ready,
and the river has loosed itself
into ruminating clarity, it has shed
ice edges.

I cannot cross this river,
we are both too sanctified.

V
August is the cruel month,
August is the month of the moon's purgation; I have
lain in effigy, I cannot stand,
I am reduced to sleep —

113 days of unbroken wilderness
113 days of silence
113 days with my seams held outward to fray, to sing.
I am born in the shuddering of the bus,
into the blanket my mother stitched.
Asleep with abstersion, asleep with words.

Death's a fierce meadowlark: but to die having made
Something more equal to the centuries
Than muscle and bone, is mostly to shed weakness.

I cross the river into the substanceless.

Leaving the Fundamental Assumptions Unexpressed

This morning there are massacres in Kurdistan,
    El Salvador, East Timor.

In Dickinson's hometown, a boy
has burned himself in protest.
I want him to be Joan of Arc —
on the pyre, triumphant, dressed in the robes of a monk,
and strong, with the strong legs of a woman.
While she burned, women read the smoke in the sky.
Some refused to spin, others broke
their cooking spoons.
Midwives sifted Joan's smouldering dust into an unguent
to ease the births of difficult children.
The boy, Gregory Levey, is this woman,
and I am at the chapel in Autun
among pilgrims, walking over stones, lighting
candles where Joan lit them.

This is a dream of solidarity.

Gregory Levey rests in the last news pages
dumped off the shelves of the magazine stand
and burned in a can
at the corner of 53rd and Avalon
where a ragged woman warms her hands
over his assumption.

Torn

The first communion is the taking
        I told him no,
Of his body into yours,
        It was my first communion,
The making of his bones into yours
        The taking of Christ's body, his blood into mine.
The moment when the worshipper becomes
        "Uncle, I won't dance with you drunk.
A part of the resurrection —
        I am dressed in
The pain and joy, the suffering, the splendor
        My new white dress. I have white shoes. And you —
Made tangible as bread and wine. Like the catfish skull
        Drunk."
My uncle kept in his living room,
        But he was angry, he wanted to dance, he wanted
The shape in the back of the skull looked like a crucifix —
        Me inside the closet, alone.
It formed a crucifix.
        I looked at the hangers.
The catfish was the dead witness
        I held onto my dress,
To the miracle of communion:
        I thought, "I am alone,
The body made into his body,
        He is not here, he is not doing this."
Bones stitched
        And I was sure something ripped
In a mystical lace. Look
        In that closet, it was my body, my blood

At the finely embroidered robes that adorn
        My fine stitched dress.
The five crosses on the altar, just like my bones,
        I looked at the hangers rising over me like ghosts
Shaped for first communion
        My body torn.
by his.

Touched

Emma who talked to angels had come
to the mountain to make an exchange.

They followed her there,
those angels she heard, who touched her

in the soft ways angels do: inside the ear,
at the collar bone, on the belly where

the hair grows to a crest. She wanted
to answer. Her husband

was a cowboy. There were words
that came into the world as he did: handle,

spur. Those words
had touched her too.

She was a dancer, moving with gravity like
surf on reefs, as the aroused mountain moves

onto the sea below. When she came to the cliff
it wasn't from fear as much as to measure

the pull of mountain towards ocean, of cowboy
leaning into saddle — the theory.

She knew the body's weight in the world,
its delicate balance, its springs. Over

the rail she tested her own gravity,
taking stock of density and drag, looking down,

like the giant she had become, on the beaches,
hills, and town reduced by her height. She lifted

her skirts. (Who wouldn't, feeling the touch,
the voices of other worlds brushing?

Who wouldn't make the crossing?) Her arms wide,
touched as she fell, her body shrinking by degrees.

Pinned

A man is reading my bones tonight,
in some kind of archaeological frenzy.
He dusts the pre-history of another's touch, sifting
my collarbones, his hand under the glass.

And I have had to pin back my hair, although it wants
to wander & spark,
it wants to fly in the face
of his fancy manners
& be unwed, unvalued,
unavailable for comment.

I would like to be
always unpinned,
so that even the certain fingers of the blind
cannot decipher my selves,
I would like to go on meaning
the meanings of my bones
la parole vive
the letters of clavicle & winged hips, not fixed
but coiling, their hollow cups unfolding,
saying & saying,
my hair unbraiding itself
without direction.

In Vezelay, I saw the bones
of the Magdalene held
beneath the high hips of Gothic arches
in a vault, in a vessel, adorned
with velvet & gold.
The message:
we have the whore,

she is sold, she is glass & velvet,
she is stone.

My body
in its case
refuses him the tools of his trade:
thin-handled hammer, magnifying
glass, the hands.

Welfare Blues

I have wanted to write you this welfare
poem — to tell you I am faring
well in spite
        of you, though I am lazy
and could easily find a job if I tried,
I prefer to use the government.
I prefer to sponge
        the floors of city buildings,
to mop the stalls of government,
to earn my full well
fare cheque. The cheque you divide by the minimum
wage to calculate the hours I must lick
envelopes telling other lazywelfarescum
their cheques have
been cut
        in line to talk to you
welfare agent, who, if you don't come on to me,
having the knowledge of my file,
might decide I haven't tried
to find a job, and besides,
my kids don't look clean, at least not as clean as your
floors when I am through.

Twin

They took her in their hands
and made her do it, made her
make them
come. They said *do it*, and she did
because her own life surfaced
inside, saying this I will carry too,
her own life buoyed up, a raft in drunken seas.
They were not evil, they were
her friends, holding her hands,
holding her head
one at a time, children passing a ball
back and forth.
The foot of one on her stomach,
they knelt over her, in the mud, in the woods,
under trees that hid
the moon, straining to shine through.
She swallowed her pride until

> some part of her
> (though it was not her aching mouth
> raw throat   that tongue that bulged to fill her scream)
> some part, rattling inside like the angry moon

> lifted
> > (she dreamt her teeth fell out
> > each tooth shrinking from the gum
> > each tooth dropped from its root like icicle
> > knocked from eave
> > teeth she would leave
> > on her pillow)

> lifted up

till there were two of her

    and they let go,
    stumbling backwards, away from her staring
    at their dirty knees, fingers fumbling at the fly,
    staring at their bent heads, she looked down,
    an angel pressed in the mud.

Long Distance

Your voice tonight,
pulsing the wire,
deep note,
rough edge —
forgotten vein of my body.

Remember how you loved
the idea of corpse?

You wanted to know the Latin words
(an early valentine named the heart's
ventricles).

Once I told you
the heart of a fetus
beat with its mother's heart.
Separated, we would know each other
by our synchronous pulse.

Now this pulmonary pause,
this apprehension,
What do you want?

Carrying Place

I brought us here
to a new country, new family,
believing there would be space enough,
we had been confined too long on island.

I brought us from prairies and oceans,
both a semaphore for loneliness,
to the seam between them, where roads
hold a dialogue between different
kinds of things. Here is
a place to squat, draw my shawl
around my shoulders, to count
what I have for trade.

People gather.
See what I have for barter:
seeds, clean paper, an instrument's strings,
a green cloth that held my children when I bent
at a crossing to scoop them from dark rooms.

If we carried other things, other names,
there might be a place for us, away
from the din, the endless banging of the sea
on the steps that lead
from the water to the land.
There might be answers, forms to fill out,
places to hold an account, to account for us,
to hold our pieces, our children.

Here we have carrying place,
common ground.
I wave the green cloth to say
these are my belongings.

Fall

On these nights that fall early
when leaves drop, mottled,
like the wings of insects who die
in the name of summer,
on these days when flames lick
the iron teeth of grates,
when women swathe themselves in dark cloth
and begin to save eggs, when everything is preserved
against the possibility of decay,
I crawl inside the tenuous nest of sleep.

Things grow uncertain. Plots change.
You have said you will always love me,
but your back is out, your face is framed
with the look of one who got away.
We have spent hours together tying
the tomatoes to wooden stakes
with a twine so frail it cannot promise
anything. We watch the same movies
over and over
knowing all endings are subject to change,
in the way that leaves will drain
their chlorophyll revealing red.

The characters turn
mean, a woman's murderer
may be her fiancé, may be
the detective, the clock hands
change place,
and we are falling back onto a new hour
that darkens early.
Your attention strays.
All my clothing grows sleeves and legs.

I am bound to my neck in wool
when I step outside to recover
the few left in nests
made of twigs and string
who wait for a body to deliver them
from the fall.

Dog Notes

How could I burn two things in a row?
Turned to ash under the broiler
        (toaster's broke)
and the dog's still barking at
yesterday's window parade.
I burned these two: toast and you.
Dog can hardly see through glass.
Barking.

Waking at night to eyelid's wall,
        (dog shifts sensing I am conscious)
I cannot discern his form in the blue bruise
of air between us.
How we cloud our own vision.
For a moment this: I will always be
squinting, trying to find the edge of things.

Tongued again after a night's sweat!
Dog tireless in his salt pursuit;
I am no one's wife, but Lot's.

Through the pane he watches work
men slug trenches in the road,
dig pipes and wires, dirt and lines;
steaming tar sucks into
house, nostrils, throat.
They're burying communication.

Unravelling

What arose as I drove to the river's mouth
was a knot made of roads leading to you.
Following the arrow
of highway lines
towards the moment we would hold each other,
I thought of our last
meeting — your hesitations, glances
in another direction.
As I drove, I saw the highway's other side,
what's in the rearview mirror, a time
when the quick of your breath in the phone
would not call me out to see
you, my voice would not carry you
from sea to shore.
I knew we would begin to unravel.
Like the ship that cannot name the moment
it has passed the river's mouth
we would turn
from each other.
It was an old movie of how we came
to love each other
played backwards, until all those times
you pulled me towards you
seemed to be the moment when two lovers part,
the light on the screen showing between their bodies,
their mouths moving towards other purposes,
as one heading out to sea will turn
at the break
water away from the shore.

Then

for Jonathan Green

Then there was the night in the Burgundy Valley
we drove the Quatre-L in the rain.
Wiper blades clearing a blurred V, shoulder
blades hunched over the steering wheel.

Thatched roofs, dirt street,
fourteenth-century madonnas
miraculous, bleeding rain.

Where sunflowers grew,
a man in black tie, refusing a ride,
led us through the village to the *grillée*.
A cow, a child watched.

I will forget prayers,
dogs I have sung to,
the maiden name of my grandmother,
but never the angle of your elbow tipped
in rain.

And you were singing Bob Dylan then,
and even then,
I ached for the girl, and the cow,
and the tuxedoed man shrouded in a towel,
and even then for you.

The Cell

I take back what I said
that made you leave the room.
How could I hurt you
without meaning to? I snap each word
back into my mouth,
like the letters of a typewriter flying back
into place. I take back
yesterday when I jerked the dog's leash,
now I let him leap away from me.
I take back everything,
the children.
Take back the summer I left home
slept in my car between the seats
on the emergency brake.
I take back him
and him and him.
I take back high school (who was
I then?). Adolescence is gone,
erased, the breasts dissolve under my blouse.
And the girl in fifth grade I bit
when she tried to steal my library book?
I remove each tooth from her arm,
and wipe off the bruise, a ghoulish, green ring.
I take back the time I teased the boy
shorter than me, the one who couldn't wrestle.
I take back the mud pond
where I ruined the shirt my grandmother made,
I swallow each dried grain
till the shirt is blue again.
The prayers I made my sister say.
>   On swollen knees, we pleaded
>   for forgiveness.

I take back my legs, my arms, my tongue,

the bones and muscles, one by one.
I take my father out of my mother
each speck flying back into him,
he slurps them up. I sit,
the blood-red egg cell
alone, tempting

The Split

All kinds of tables list the tortures
we give one another.

In your 5′ 8″ frame, soft skull,
and the tufts of old hair,
you tell me the spheres sing to us,
while the demons of new physics count down
our cadence. It's a crueller lullaby,
a radioactive splitting
that goes on between you
and me, because you cannot name yourself,
because you are dying,
your body is dying,
your half-life overcome, splitting:
these double meanings, duplicitous words,
explaining ways of being
in two places at once,
two hearts at once, two cunts at once.
You are nuclear family
to me, love canal, the 800 building reactor
that employs 3,000 to shut it
down, to clean it out,
to erase the touch of
strontium   deutirium   uranium
ore, the haunt of atoms split, while we made
love over the nucleus,
the isotopic truth,

till we were flashed and then annihilated
till there were only photographs of our outlines.

Little boy, dying your crumbling
old man death. I am a halogen girl,
brillant with the shine of light.
You cannot hold me.

Snapshot

What made me mad was the picture.
The snapshot I had of you
in my kitchen, cutting onions
for a pot of ragout.
It was a good dinner — you with that grinning
face, making love to the camera
and everyone else.

But it's the snapshot that made me mad.
That I had it in my head,
that face of yours halfway
around the world. On the airplane, it fell
between my pillow
and the ashtray. On the beach,
it lay in the sand.
The stupid sand that came back
with me too, in the cracks of my skin
in the gapes of my shoes.

Halfway around the globe
and I had to shake the sand from your
hand on the knife.

Epaulettes

I've been struck twice by lightning —
certain restaurants refuse to serve me
during storms.

I've set off airport detectors
with the fillings in my teeth or the bb pellet
lodged in my bone by a soldier of fortune.

I've crossed customs at night
carrying too many pets and tropical plants,
had them turn me away because of my shoulder sag,

as though my body is
my credit rating,
my passport.

Knowing what the body carries,
how we can be marked by scars,
I wear mine

with some majesty, as the commander
of a large fleet.
I wear my body

as one accustomed to battles,
to cruelties. I boast
with each shocked extremity.

Loosestrife

I am looking in the rearview
mirror, thinking of you, who left
what you could behind,
where I see purple, where I see blue,
bruised view. My mirror thick
with loosestrife,
the plant whose root,
like a lover's tongue, drains
the soil of its necessary wet. A weed
with a greedy, purple thirst.

No matter the children,
their budding breasts, their creamy,
fresh sex, even though they knife the roots
from the ground, this loosestrife
has buried itself
in the heart of the heart
land, in the heart of the wetland.
Like you, when I was new, before
I could push you out,
you left me
looking back.

LOVE'S BACK

for Douglas

After the Drought

Until this year I didn't know the shapes
and tastes of these trees. The coded branches

held a dream of heavy fruit. In the rain
that fell we were all dripping

throats. Trees tilted back their necks, stealing sweet
from the mouth of morning. In my backyard

the calla lily cups her hand to possess
the wet luxury. It rains at six,

the ground is dry by nine. Even
the concrete blooms. Colour

has cracked into this OZ.
Walking home along the tilted

sidewalks, my ankles trade in seeds, knock
dandelions from their stems,

scratch the legs of buds
who have pushed through darkness.

From the tree an offering
in orange: I taste a language, Body.

Your Touch

In other centuries, other creatures'
fantasies, on a prehistoric day dense
with heat, some small mammal
brushed the neck of its mate
and ushered in our possibility.

When you have found the place
between my shoulder and
my head, that tough band
that runs in my family
up the neck, you will reach through
the veil of my hair, and press
the weight of history
upon my skin.

You will touch me and
I will remember my first lesson
in evolution: in caves there are fish
who have lost their eyes.
In the dark grottos, the deep waters
they need only touch.

Builders poised on the upper beams
of a tower hauling themselves
into the immaculate
openness of space,
we push into each other, blind
to the future we penetrate.

Early Morning

The morning of the funeral we woke early.
There was no reason
for it, we had time to shower, to dress —
we had time to sleep.
But there was something in the air
gushing off the grass,
there was something in the scent
of the soil
that woke us.

At noon we would bury another friend,
another one betrayed by love
of the shoot,
of growing things.

We would lay him in a plot
of earth, as if there were
a justly unravelling thread
that led him to his end.
As if we could make sense of this.
Forced to rise,

we rose,
our green selves unfurling,
every cell of us ripe,

stretching, you rooted
yourself in me,
a blossom in rebellion
for this man, for desire
buried in the seed of him.

But Only the Captains of This Earth

The captain himself fashioned this busk,
shaped it from whalebone —

and he will be gone three years
while I wait in the tight jaws

of the beast, my body stowaway
in a landlocked ship.

I wake to the sound of someone scrubbing
the sea wall, cleaning obscene life

from its pores. Who is the captain
of the body that moves me?

Days, the sun shines before me
like a doubloon. Nights, I craft

the vessel of my own longing. Boiling
the skeleton, tugging thick cartilage,

cutting in — block and tackle strung overhead.
Alone, I scrape meat from bones to excavate architecture,

the plan of another artist. Lying along
the vertebrae, inside ivory ribs, I build myself

into the animal, a scrimshaw hull,
ornate, jointed,

fashioned for departure.

Broad Reach

I expect bespectacled love
to talk himself into my heart.
Then you arrive,
back square to the squall,
three days stubble,
and a passion for compasses.
Maybe it's the chisel of your nose and throat,
your shrug that falls off the wind
onto broad reach,
that allows me
to give you
                'my heart to chart.'
I thought love would be scholarly,
but you are this unruly ocean,
sounding, bearing.

Love's Back

I am trying to know this beast
that breathes through its back, trying
to understand its
gargoyle ways.
I have to work from the centre
out, I have to learn it
from the bones' blueprints.

What I do not know is this:
what it thinks, what it means,
whether it has slept
or if it dreams, whether it is passionate or cruel.
I do not know its fears or its pain.
I do not know its underwater ways.

I know the whale only
by its back, the strange
in and out of its breath,
brief moisture of its kiss.
Of what lover can we say anything else?

Storm Room

Once this room held
only me. Its ceilings and its walls
were shaped to your absence.

Each space had the quality of a forest
when a rainstorm has passed
before the first bird sounds.

When you came, the room bent
inward. Everything leaned
towards your frame. Every depression

in the furniture, even the hollow of my bed
bulged with the bulk of you.
The house renovated.

Tonight just as someone spoke
your name, you brushed
my arm, your fingers sparking the hairs.

They stood at attention.
My body, so like a house, opened itself, moved
in your direction.

Let's face it.
You were not there.
It was only a name on his lips.

It was a stranger who brushed me. You
left the house,
nothing weights the rooms.

Detail from Storm Room

The forest grows deep stands
of trees, rich, thick, more colours of green
than there are words to name them.
The eye hungers
for release from this lush,
the hush of sunlight splayed through
branches. Where is the rain
that fell before, where
is the weight that filled the place?
Pools and cups brimming,
leaves slick, wet — the storm has passed
and in its place there is an empty quality
like the feeling of being without
you. The noise of your absence
has replaced the rain.
Then
                                        two-we-two, a bird sounds.

Detail from Detail from Storm Room

two-we-two

Mercury, a Quick Note to You

I think you must be back in Boston
between pale leaves and hints of snow,
or is it snowing already? The city thick
in it, cars trudging and feet heavy.

I'm in Canada.
Nights, dog yowls through the glass
at the ankle of moon
dangling over the trees.
Days, its cars, their gawdy
plumage a reason to bark.

The snow's already blanketing here.
A convenient white lie, it covers the place.
We seek colour anywhere or paralysed,
search for cover, build fires,
crouch inside frozen rooms.

I think you must be busy in your laboratory.
Mixing sauces with names you have
repeated to me in sleep. Do you
play with mercury? The shine like moon
on water or glass sliding along a counter,
shattering into beads that pool together
the way bodies can.
Mixing your silver potions, your drams,
do you think of me?

I will not wait for snow to melt
its tiny petals turned to water, I will
not wait for moon to break.

And if I make my way
down the corridor between shelves of glass,
vials, flasks, if I do come to find you, at last,
will you be silver cold or will you spill
yourself towards me?
Will you melt?

    yours,   e.

Scales

I wanted to believe
in weight, the globe
on the shoulders of Atlas,

but for me the world was
nothing, it was empty
except for light.

I wanted teeth
and tongues, but found
only syllable and sound —

I could not trust objects,
trying to understand a man by his boot print
instead of his boot.

You came, having lifted engine blocks,
touched rivets and a newborn's skull,
you who hold the world

like a lens, bending
its light, shaping its light,
focusing immaterial

into weight that I can believe in.
Cut ice is the mark of a steel
skate, a body has bulk

and leaves a print in the snow.
Why not trust these belongings?
Why not bend hesitation?

You were fed on oceans, on fish
whose scales are fine lenses
catching light scattered

by the sea; you were nursed on the border
between water and land, on food salty
and immaculate.

What the Cookbook Doesn't Say

Soak the dogfish in lemon juice to neutralize —
One half teaspoon for each pound of meat.
            — The Dogfish Cookbook

The night after the slaughter, I was underwater,
I could breathe.
Drenched with salt,
I waited for your brief
touch across the sheets,
your hand in the bucket of the bed.

I had watched you on the stones
beside the sea, press the heads of dogfish
onto nails driven into carving boards.

Up to your elbows in blood,
the filleting knife
gripped in your webbed fingers,
with the other hand
you pulled the living pups
from their mother's gut,
releasing them into the bucket.
At once, butcher, midwife.

My desire explained
in the baked heat of the rocks,
between the bodies of dogfish:
I am torn
born in your hands.

Moving In

We begin to have the same dreams.
Yours are of fish, huge silent herds
moving through dark waters.

This is because you are returning
to school. You will study fish,
the lateral lines,
how the slightest touch
can move the direction of the whole,
how they lead each other from what
would devour them, how
they seem to be one fish.

I accept this — my head on the pillow
touching yours. Your dreams leap upstream.
I can hardly dream without the flash
of scales in reflected light, the dapple
of us moving side by side.

In the past, I dreamt of a hook
or of little fish in the belly
of big fish in the belly
of biggest.

But I like this: one body
made from many
moving together.

How I Came to Know the Woman in Him

Apples. Red as a pick-up,
smooth and uninvited, or red as the quilt
on the single bed.
Offered through the burnished
leaves, passed down between branches.
I would accept our exile.

Hands. The way she splits fruit, the care of thumbnail
carving groove — how the seeds fall
between two halves: me, you.

Gills. Caught by hook and gaff
when the fish is brought
into the boat, its open wounds opened wide,
its mouth mouthing Os.
She says, *this I chose for you*.

Cup. Opening and closing me, the cup
of water left at bedside. Inside the water,
filaments, static electricity.
Between atoms: the hum
of her name.
The source of my thirst, my delight.
She fills rooms with rooms (life with life).

Throat. It moves against the will of other bones,
against the proclivities of silence;
the knees of crickets rub,
she speaks.

When she makes love to me, no red wound
or gash, no absence, just the prayer against silence,
the slow heaving of the giant sea, splitting
at the seams.

Fractal Lover

It happens when you spend
all afternoon splitting wood.
Each cellulose cell stiffens to your work,
the axe in the air,
poised possibility.

You carry down the arc
of your attention, intention
revealed by the blade
that parts the log.

All afternoon, splitting
wood, the snow heaving itself down
like so many ashes from cold
fires, you force your axe into the air
                                    answering the snow.

I am inside burning
wood, remembering
ways I have been split, how you will come
into the room the cold air a signature
around you, how you will crack me

in ways my body knew when its first cells
unchained their rosary,
made themselves again,

opening the branches
of guanine   adenine   thymine
cytosine   uncoupling the links

it happens with stiff industry
this pairing repeats.

Daughter Imagined

At night, when the low moon fills
my room, I dream the unnamed girl.

Reckless,
even as an infant, she will climb too high,
walk too soon.
She will ride upside
down on a rollercoaster, arms hanging over her head,
her head hanging down
as it did at birth.
She will coast over train tracks
after the barrier has gone down,
the lights clanging and flashing, her bicycle skidding
between the tracks. She will throw herself
into life's wheels
so completely that I hold my breath. Wait
for telephone calls.
Say all the things my mother said.

Soon her father will come to me
with the same intensity, and she will leap
into our lives
before we can stop her.

Le Rêve

I woke from turbulent sleep to the smell
you had gathered. Lilies, Le Rêve
you told me, in your serious voice,
a flower too, sweating nectar, blooming moon.
And the lilies were closed —
tight lips, pink blush, the Younger Sister
of Exclamation, shy in their longing.
But today to awake and find them,
fine Antigones,
speckled tongues waving, singing with pollen,
petals arched, and the perfume,
oh, the smell,
your voice calling me from sleep to dream.

Shipbuilding

Our own bones slipped,
as we repaired the whale's bones,
assembled the pieces of its body.
Fixed with concentration, looking
with glass-rimmed eyes, my hands
held the bones together
while you spread hardeners and glues.
Still, our interlaced fingers fumbled —
we could not mimic the construction of this creature

or the one in me. Half-formed
and thoughtless, she sped
towards tidier ends,
working with different substances:
the body's adhesives, its glues. Each cell
strained to form the next.
No wire webs or planks, only chemical
links — my belly swelling,
my blood transformed into this small, blind builder
who constructed her own eyes,
built from inside a scaffolding
to hold her own.

Who were we to try this mystical, this fine work
that infants do?

When she was born, I hoisted
my frame. I opened the world to her.
Lifting my hips, releasing this vessel
from the berth I once built.

My Epileptic

My epileptic was born after
the moon landing. An alien alighting
in a world of television.

At night he dreamt of global insurrection,
of secret groups in rags. Sucking drugs
slipped between gums and tongue,
he fell into febrile sleep,

his body an alarm ringing
with concentration.

His father said he was a natural disaster,
his own fault,
his own quake.
But I gave him his body,
and in his body, he held my terror
of nuclear hybrids, toxic waste.
He was the strain of my womb.

He would swing, pendulous, even in sleep,
the ground swollen and shifting
under floors that he dreamed —
head between his knees in the gymnasium,
my epileptic burnt, and shook,

sounded an alarm against his own
planet, his own darkness.

Airborne

Our son in the air
floating over you,
stomach on your feet,
legs and arms, tail and wings.
You flung him up, said, *see birds,*
clouds like beards, see tops of trees?
Our son overhead, an Icarus crying, *Fly me higher.*
The bed, an escarpment,
ancient land pushed up by glaciers. The bedroom strewn
with clothes, shoes, books,
under his body, our topography unravels,
a fertile country where fathers hold
the secret of gravity.
You point your toes, he soars, his skin shiny,
his eyes, windows too small for his body.

I know the forces that landed him here. You
put yourself around me lifting
off, saying grab my wings.
I never trusted flying, hung on
for dear life.

North

We headed north.
We packed our bags, cooler,
grabbed the camera, dog, children.
After everything,
we headed north.

Tuned to the sounds
of cities, machines, laser beams.
It was the end of the century, end of
the millennium, a hot July day,
we scanned the sky
for change, cloudbreak.

On the road, we dodged each leaf
we thought was a frog,
stopped to swim, wet dry July skin
in the arms of rivers
that pour from Arctic waters.

You sang to me about your childhood,
Every bone on my plate was a gift.
I learned to tell time by the sun
on the dash,
the miles peeling back.
There were only dirt roads.

Getting gas: the man behind the register rubs his chin
offers water to the dog, soda to the kids,
weather predictions. You talk fishing with him
debate bait,
tackle tackle, floats, spins
the conversation weaves between you,
a net pulling in breathless afternoon air.

Then we are off again.
Off to the whales,
to swim with them
after so many miles. They will eye us,
creatures from another world,
we will eye them.

Though we wear false skin, we will move
with the living animal,
immersed in its element, spy on
its vast migration — the whale carries
all it has and knows with it.
We will learn its way to swim.

The road north. Follow it. Sing.
Fall in a new trajectory:
every leaf, a frog
every crow, a fisherman
each child, a creature shedding skin.

Prepare for the whale,
the secrets of the body
how to carry place with you
in times of migration.

Notes

1. In its January 1993 edition, *Outside Magazine* published an article documenting the death of twenty-four-year-old Christopher McCandless. McCandless, who called himself Alexander Supertramp, had left his family two years earlier after signing over his $20,000 trust fund to the Oxford Famine Relief Fund. He was last seen alive on Tuesday, April 28, 1992, when he entered the Alaska wilderness. One hundred and thirteen days later, he was found dead on the edge of the Denali National Park in an abandoned bus. The italics are excerpts from Christopher's journals, found with his body, and from books that he used as writing paper.

2. The title "Leaving the Fundamental Assumptions Unexpressed" comes from Noam Chomsky's *Language and Politics*.

3. Carrying Place is a town in southern Ontario.

4. The title "But Only the Captains of This Earth" comes from Herman Melville's *Moby Dick*.

5. "Love's Back" comes from the Sharon Olds line "I know love when I see its back."

6. The dogfish is a shark that gives birth to live young.

7. The poem "How I Came to Know the Woman in Him" is after Bruce Smith's poem "How You Came into My Hands."

8. A fractal is a shape that exhibits self-similarity on all scales.

Acknowledgements

Thanks, first of all, to my editor Anne Szumigalski for her patience and guidance. Thanks also to Martha Sharpe and Michael B. Davis at Anansi. I am indebted to Janice Kulyk Keefer for her thoughtful reading of the first draft. Many people read the manuscript or parts of the manuscript before it went to the press: Michael Ondaatje, Linda Spalding, Douglas Fudge, Michael Redhill, Griffin Ondaatje, Kristin Spalding, Roo Borson, Bruce Smith, Annie Carr, and Jeremy Robins. Thanks to all for their generosity. For their inspiration, thanks to the young writers at the Andover-Lawrence Writer's Workshop. A special thanks to my first reader, Constance Rooke, who told me I could, and to my father, Philip, for his eyes.

Even by the sea that we love with its breaking . . . we cannot tell you what to take with you. — W. S. Merwin
Much love and thanks to my mother, Linda, and to Michael. You showed me what to carry.

"Under the Blankets" and "Backyard Growing Up" are for Kristin. "Then" is for Jonathan Green. "Broad Reach" is for Jim Brogden.

This book was written with the support of several Ontario Arts Council Writer's Reserve Grants. Thanks to Brick Books, Cormorant Books, and *Arc*.

Some of these poems have appeared in a slightly different form in the following magazines: *A Room of One's Own, CV2, Fiddlehead, Fireweed, Grain, The Malahat Review, McGill Street Magazine, The Muse Journal,* and *Prairie Fire*.